For Danni Corgan – J.W.

Read more in this online-safety series by Jeanne Willis and Tony Ross:

Chicken Clicking

Troll Stinks

#Goldilocks: A Hashtag Cautionary Tale

First published in Great Britain in 2021 by Andersen Press Ltd.,
20 Vauxhall Bridge Road, London SW1V 2SA.
Text copyright © Jeanne Willis, 2021.
Illustration copyright © Tony Ross, 2021.
The rights of Jeanne Willis and Tony Ross to be identified
as the author and illustrator of this work have
been asserted by them in accordance with the
Copyright, Designs and Patents Act, 1988.
All rights reserved.
Printed and bound in China.
First edition.
British Library Cataloguing in Publication Data available.
ISBN 978 1 78344 952 1

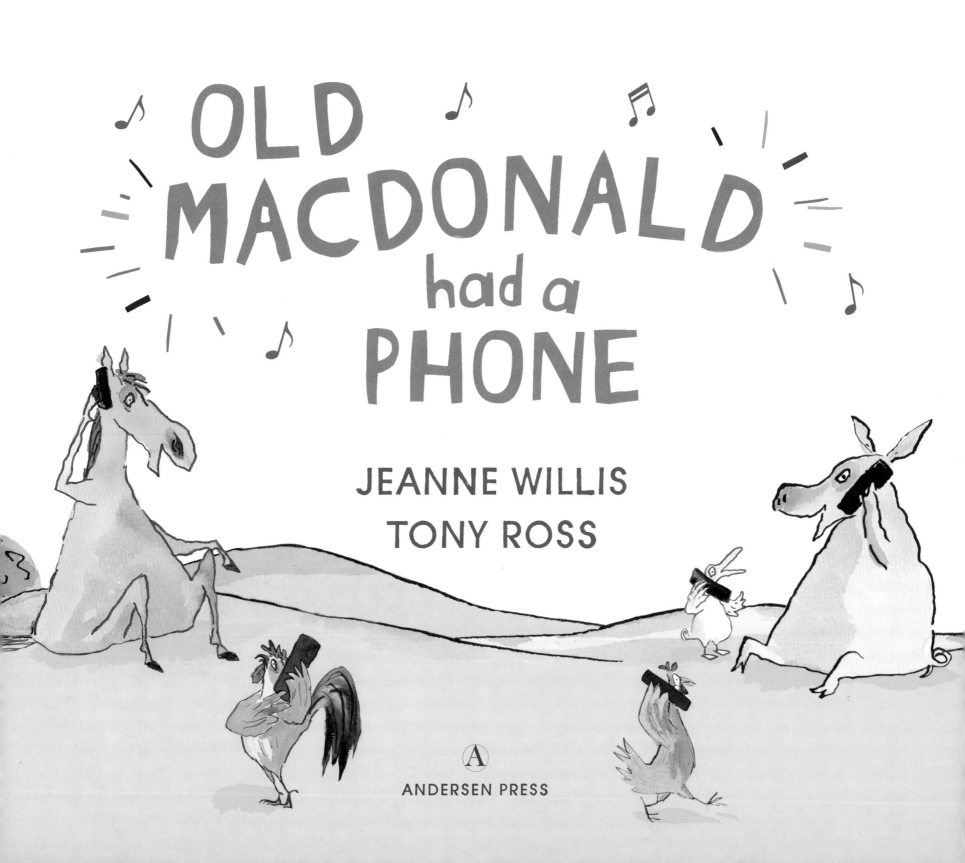

OLD MACDONALD had a PHONE

JEANNE WILLIS

TONY ROSS

ANDERSEN PRESS

♫ ♪ Old Macdonald had a phone ♫ ♪

And it was very smart,

It helped him organise his farm
And fill his shopping cart...

♫ Old Macdonald had a phone ♪
He dropped it in the lake.

He ordered one online but...

Bought a hundred by mistake!

They were taken by the cows,
The boars and the sows,
The rooster, sheep and hens
And all their furry friends.

♪ ♪ Everybody had a phone ♫
And it was such good fun!

Nobody would put them down
So nothing else got done.

 The rooster didn't crow,

The horse wouldn't go...

The sheep ignored the rams,
The sheepdog lost the lambs.

Old Macdonald had a farm
But nothing in his shop,

Cows messaging at milking time
Would not produce a drop.

♪ The hens wouldn't lay, ♫
On their phones all day,

Here a tweet, there a chat,
WhatsApping the farm cat.

Old Macdonald used to run
The noisiest of farms,
Now all he hears are ring tones
And the beep of phone alarms.

Old Macdonald took the phones
And locked them in the shed,
It made the sheepdog so annoyed,
He sulked and went to bed.

The fox scared the sheep,

The rooster stayed asleep,

The bull refused to sweep
His manure in a heap...

Young Macdonald found his dad
Sobbing in his van,
"Smart phones aren't
so bad," he said.
"Get with the times, old man."

"Like all technology,
If we use it sensibly
And live life to the full,
Then phones are cool."

They had a meeting at the farm
With all the animals,
And promised to give back the phones
If they obeyed these rules:
A chat-chat here, and a selfie there,
But not all day! Does that sound fair?

♪ The creatures at Macdonald's Farm ♫
Agreed with what was said.
They limited their phone time,
And they ran the farm instead.

♪ The eggs were laid, ♪

The milk was made...

They all had a party
Now the bills were paid!

♪ ♫ All the creatures on the farm ♫
Are happy as can be,
They talk to one another
And they do not text at tea.

Lots of little pigs

And lambs are born...

♫ Best of all, Macdonald's bull ♪
Won first prize in the show,

And everybody texted...

Smiley Face, YOLO! YOLO!